蜜ぱら

恋渕ももな
Koibuchi MOMONA

Koibuchi
MOMONA
PHOTO BOOK
Location in Thailand

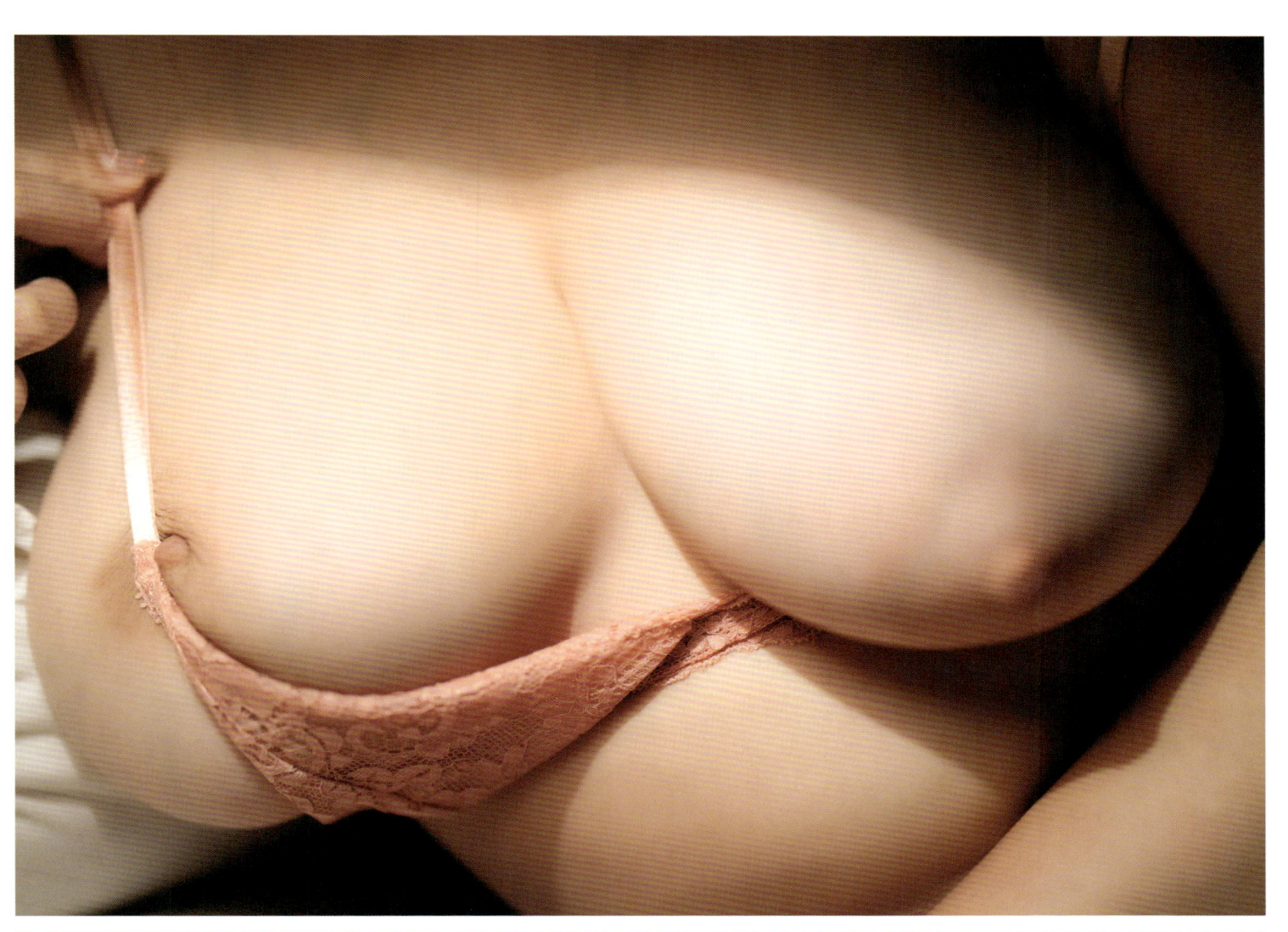

Koibuchi MOMONA
PHOTO BOOK
Location in Thailand

Artist: KOIBUCHI MOMONA
Photographer: MAKIHARA SUSUMU
Styling: TOSHIKUNI ISAKO
Hair and make-up: TOSHIKUNI ISAKO
Artist Management: TAKAHASHI MITSUHIRO (LIFE PROMOTION)
　　　　　　　　　　YOSHIDA TOMOKI (LIFE PROMOTION)
Art Director: MIZUKI RYOTA
Editor: SHIBATA HIROSHI (TAKESHOBO)

Printed in JAPAN
©2025 Takeshobo Co.,Ltd.